SNOWED IN BITE

S.J. TILLY

This book is dedicated to my friend G. Marie and her novella Snowed in Fling.
I hadn't realized I was using basically the same title as you until it was too late.
Thank you for being chill and sharing the vibes.

Chapter One

ALICE

I squeeze Michael's hand, and his dark eyes lower to meet mine.

He squeezes my hand back. "What is it, Baby Cakes?"

I roll my lips together and tip my head just the smallest bit to the side.

Michael's mouth pulls up on one side. "I need more than that, Sweetie."

Sweetie. Gah.

I can't believe any of this.

Literally none of it.

The last few days have been a total dream. A whirlwind. A fairytale.

But today... reality is setting in, and I don't quite know how to handle it.

I keep my voice low as I point out the obvious. "Everyone is staring."

He doesn't miss a beat. "I know. I can't keep my eyes off you either."

My cheeks heat at his insinuation that people are staring at me. But we both know that's not true. They're looking at him.

Michael is literally famous, and I'm nobody.

Well, not nobody. Not after the live-streamed episodes of

Second Bite that played around the world three days in a row, ending yesterday.

Before that, no one had ever heard of me, but now I'm Alice Hatter, contestant from the *Second Bite* holiday special, who did fine on the first challenge, spectacularly screwed up the second challenge, got a Chef Mike Kesso Second Bite on the third challenge, and embarrassed herself more than once—stumbling over words and feet, for the world to see.

I didn't win. Not with my ice cream atrocity.

So yeah, I'm just the girl from the show.

Not the winner. Just a girl.

Now, if the world had seen the rest of the stuff that happened after the cameras turned off... like Michael coming to my hotel room and shoving his face under my skirt...

If the public knew about that, the stares would probably be wider.

Michael squeezes my fingers, and my pulse flutters through my body.

I never expected that *the Chef Mike Kesso* would end up as in love with me as I am with him.

I never could have guessed that Michael would return my years-long obsession the moment he laid eyes on me.

I never dreamed my life would change because of a television show.

But it did.

And now here we are.

Together.

In public.

And not just public but the Minneapolis International Airport, holding hands, for everyone to see.

I dart my eyes around, confirming that, yes, many people are still staring at Chef Mike, TV personality and world-renowned baker.

A man who has been famous for years. Decades honestly.

And at forty-five, fifteen years my senior, he's only gotten better looking.

His masculine jawline, his salt-and-pepper features, his tattoos, his bad-boy attitude, his strong, skilled hands...

My cheeks start to heat for a whole other reason as I think of him naked, grunting and gripping me to him while his weight drives me into my mattress.

"What are you thinking of now?" His deep voice rumbles over me.

I blink up at him. "Nothing."

His grip on my hand shifts so our fingers are entwined. "You're a terrible liar."

I huff. "Don't change the subject."

"And what exactly was the subject?"

"You know." I widen my eyes. "The staring."

"Ah, yes. That."

"What do we do about it?" I ask.

Michael's smile is soft. "Nothing."

"But—"

"You'll learn to ignore it," he says like that will be easy. Like having a large percentage of the population looking at us isn't a big deal. "Come on, let's grab some breakfast."

"Breakfast?" I'm hardly one to turn down food, but nerves are eating at my stomach.

Michael uses his grip on my hand to guide me toward a sign for a bakery in the main part of the terminal. "We'll have a meal on the plane, but I'm hungry now." He smirks at me. "You wore me out last night."

I bump his hip with our joined hands. "Michael," I admonish.

"What?" He feigns innocence.

Out of the corner of my eye, I see someone taking a photo.

I do my best to ignore it.

I really do.

But I'm not a huge fan of photos. And maybe that's because

candid photos of me always seem to be taken from the worst possible angles. Or maybe it's because I've always felt a little too big, always felt like my body takes up too much space in an image.

Really, it's probably because of a whole slew of things—society, childhood bullies, nineties movies...

But now, next to this tall, handsome man, I'm even more aware of my flaws. And even more stressed about my appearance than usual.

"Alice." Michael's tone is concerned, and I look up to see him frowning down at me.

"I'm okay." I try to soothe him.

"You tensed up. That's not okay." He stops walking and turns to face me, putting his back to the people passing, blocking everyone but him from my view. "I won't ever let anyone hurt you." He doesn't let go of my hand but lifts his free one to grip my shoulder reassuringly. "And my fans aren't like that, they won't do anything to you. But they will want to take photos. And, for the record, I want them to." He leans in a little closer. "So tell me the truth, Baby. What's wrong."

Take photos.

"You want them to take photos?"

He nods. "Of us together, yes. Now tell me what's wrong."

"I..." I don't know how to word this in a way that won't sound like I'm just fishing for compliments. "I just don't want to cause you problems," I say quietly.

He moves even closer. "How could you possibly cause me problems?"

I shrug, trying to brush it off, but I know I need to say it. "I don't want to ruin... your image." I gesture at him. "You're you. All handsome and fancy, and I'm..." I huff out a breath as my shoulders slump a bit. "I don't look like your exes." I swallow down the words that want to jump out, and gesture down my body at the gray scoop-neck dress my cousin gifted me because she didn't wear it much. "I'm wearing a secondhand dress."

I hate to bring up his exes, but I've seen them. He's a celebrity; everyone's seen them.

Michael has never been portrayed as a player, but he wasn't a virgin when he crawled over me last night. And the women he's been photographed with haven't been plus-size girlies. They've been... *not* plus-size girlies.

His chest expands as he takes a deep breath, and I brace myself for his reply.

But instead of speaking, he walks forward. Into me. Forcing me backward.

My mouth opens, but Michael shakes his head. "Not another word out of that pretty little mouth."

My jaw snaps shut.

After a few steps, Michael grips my shoulders and turns me around.

I don't try to defy him, keeping the pace he's set. But then I see that he's walking us toward the bathrooms.

Correction, he's walking us toward the single door for the private family bathroom, between the men's and women's restrooms.

A green light is illuminated next to the handle, letting us know it's empty.

"Michael," I hiss, trying to slow.

But he keeps a palm on my back, pushing me forward.

His large hand reaches past me and opens the door, then he applies more pressure on my back, urging me inside.

Since trying to resist him will cause more of a scene, I step into the small room.

Michael's oversized presence pushes in behind me, and I swear I hear some snickers and gasps before the door clicks shut.

I spin around, my mind flashing to all the dirty things that could happen behind a locked door. "Michael, we cannot have sex in an airport!"

Michael's angry expression doesn't go anywhere. "We could, Sweet Cheeks, but that's not the reason I brought you in here."

"Then why—"

He takes a step closer. "I need to say a few things to you, and as much as I appreciate my fans, I don't need any of them recording this."

I clutch my hands in front of my stomach. "Then you should probably keep your voice down."

He nods once and steps farther into my space, lowering his voice. "Listen closely, then." He reaches out with one big palm and cups my chin, keeping my eyes on him. "My past *relationships* mean nothing. Not a single woman I've ever dated or been with compares to you. You are my everything. My fucking world. My future. And you are fucking stunning."

I swallow, and he rubs his thumb under my chin, feeling the movement.

I watch his own throat work on a swallow. "I don't want to tell you anything about the women I've... been with because as far as I'm concerned, they have been erased from my memory. And if I could delete all records of them from the internet, I'd do it. But if you need to hear me say it, I'll tell you the truth that the media didn't always cover. I like women of all sizes." He shakes his head. "I *liked* women of all sizes. Now..." He drags his eyes down my form. "Now I only like one size. Alice size. And if you need me to remind you just how fucking much I lust after your body, I'd be happy to demonstrate. Right now. And prove that we indeed can have sex in an airport."

Since the moment we met in person, Michael has done nothing but prove his loyalty to me. And even though I shouldn't need the reassurance, his words are everything I needed to hear. And with a sigh, I let the safety they bring wrap around me like the sparkly, happy garland on a tree.

A smile tugs at my mouth, and I reach up, placing my hands on his chest. "Have I told you how much I love you today?"

His intense gaze shifts from protection to affection. "Not yet."

I take a deep inhale, letting his scent fill my lungs. "I love you, Chef Michael."

Chapter Two

MICHAEL

I slide my palm around to the back of Alice's neck, feeling her soft blonde curls against the back of my hand.

"I love you too, Little Miss Christmas."

As I'd hoped, her mouth pulls up into a full smile at the nickname.

She really is my Christmas miracle. My ultimate gift. And the thought of her thinking poorly of herself, in any way, lights up every cell in my body with rage.

Alice is everything I've been looking for.

Everything I've been wishing for.

She's my salvation from loneliness.

My missing ingredient.

My better half.

And with her soft gray dress, her sparkly red earrings, and her green slip-on shoes, she couldn't look more perfect.

But if she's self-conscious about her clothing, I'll buy her an entire new wardrobe. Two, if necessary.

"Give me a kiss," I demand even as I lean down and press my lips to hers.

Alice sighs, and her peppermint breath dances across my senses until all I can focus on is the warm feeling of her mouth on mine.

Her fingers dig into my chest, clinging to my shirt.

I'm tempted to rip the buttons off and peel the fabric from my body so I can feel her hands directly on my skin. But then I remember we're in a public bathroom, and a sexy scandal isn't exactly the way I want to introduce Alice to living a life of fame. I'm hoping for something more subtle, like us walking through an airport hand in hand.

I reluctantly pull back as my dick starts to throb. "Tell me you love me again."

Alice huffs out a laugh. "I love you, you bossy boy."

I reach down to adjust myself. "Good. Now let's go get something sweet to eat."

She glances down at my hand, still on my junk, before darting her gaze right back up.

Her cheeks turn pink, but I love that she hears *something sweet to eat* and looks at my dick.

I have to adjust myself again.

My fingers tighten around my length, and I groan. "Damnit, Vixen."

"What?" She snickers.

"Should've started my morning between your legs. This flight is going to kill me."

Alice smooths my shirt with her palms. "It's just a few hours, right?"

I nod.

"And then we have a couple days for your prep time?"

I nod again, confirming that production will need some time for setup.

"Well then." She taps her fingers against my chest. "It sounds like you'll have ample time to..." The pink on her cheeks deepens. "*Get between my legs.*"

With my hand still on my dick, I can feel the twitch it gives at her words.

"Baby Cakes, you're killing me." I lower my forehead to hers.

"I came in here to set you straight, and you're gonna have me leaving with tented pants."

Alice slides her hands around to my sides, holding on to me. "Girls are lucky in that sense."

"In what sense?"

She shrugs. "You can't see how turned on I am."

The groan that rolls out of my chest is immediate. She practically admitted that she's wet for me right now. "Fucking hell, Alice. You're not helping."

I give up on my dick and wrap my arms around her shoulders, hugging her to me.

Her body relaxes against mine before she whispers, "I still can't believe this is real."

I tighten my hug. "I can't believe you're real either."

We breathe each other in, but the moment is interrupted by Alice's stomach growling.

And the sound is enough to finally get my blood flow under control.

My girl is hungry.

So I must feed her.

"Food. Then plane. Then the hotel bed until tomorrow morning," I say, stepping back and reaching for the door handle.

"Um..."

I look back at Alice's hesitation. "What's wrong?"

She glances around the room. "I think we should wash our hands."

I can't stop my smirk. "You literally only touched me."

Alice rolls her eyes. "I know, but we're in a bathroom." She scrunches her cute nose. "I can't leave a bathroom without washing my hands."

"You're fucking adorable."

She shakes her head and turns toward the sink. But the movement means I can see her grinning in the mirror.

I step up beside her and fill my palm with soap. "Who knew my dirty girl was such a clean freak."

Chapter Three

ALICE

Michael gives me a reassuring nod before he grips my hand, then pulls the door open.

I try to brace myself, sure that at least a few people would have waited, probably listening outside the door to see if they could hear anything untoward. But when we step into the main hallway, I realize I wasn't braced enough.

Over a dozen people are standing there, just a few feet away, and as before, they're staring.

Only this time, they're staring at me too.

Some of the women are grinning at me, and some look to be sizing me up, but all of them keep glancing at the man at my side.

We take another step together, allowing the door to shut behind us, then he lets go of my hand.

For one horrible half second, I think he's going to step away from me.

But he doesn't.

Of course he doesn't.

Michael moves closer until my side is pressed into his and drapes his arm over my shoulders. "Sorry, I needed to have a quick word with my woman."

My woman.

The murmurs are instant, but I can't make out any individual words because my ears are too full of fluffy snow. Because, just like that, Michael has publicly claimed me.

He said he would.

I believed he would.

But still, to hear him say it, in front of a bunch of lookie-loos, half of whom have their phones raised—probably recording— feels like a pivotal moment in my life.

"Is that Alice?" someone nearly shouts, and I startle at the volume.

Then I startle at the question.

I was just recognized.

The hand draped over my shoulder grips me possessively. "Yes, this is my Alice. And if you'll excuse us, we need to secure some breakfast before our flight."

I almost expect the crowd to complain or for someone to try and stop us, but no one does. A few lift their phones higher, but most people step back.

I do my best to take subtle inhales, working to calm my nerves, then I let Michael lead me away from the bathroom.

I keep a hold of Alice as I guide her toward the bakery I spotted when I flew into Minneapolis a few days ago.

A few days ago.

How quickly life can change.

Still walking, I lean over and press a kiss to the top of Alice's head.

I need to remember that she's new to this life of fame.

And that I dragged her into it, without giving her an option, so I need to make it worth it.

I need Alice to understand how precious she is to me.

Every day.

Alice leans into me, and I feel her slide her fingers into my pants pocket, her own way of holding me close.

I kiss her hair again.

Alice tips her face back. "What's that for?"

"I don't need a reason," I reply, and she rolls her lips together, trying to smother a smile.

Chapter Five

ALICE

This man I've fantasized about for years is even better than all my dreams, and I'm not sure how to handle it.

It's like I'm living out my own festive version of Cinderella.

I bite back the urge to grin like a complete fool as we step into line at a place called Firm Buns Bakery, and I try not to snicker at the name.

The line shuffles forward, and I rest my head against Michael's body as I read the menu board mounted behind the registers.

"Know what you'd like?" Michael's voice rumbles through his chest against my shoulder.

Reluctantly, I stand up straighter so he can hear me above the general noise of the airport.

"I'm debating between sweet and savory."

"Which ones?" His gaze moves to the menu.

"The ham and cheese hand pie, or the cranberry and cream cheese Danish." My mouth practically waters as I say it.

"And to drink?"

"I can just have water." My eyes roam to the prices. "Or I can just stop at the drinking fountain."

Michael's chest rises with what can only be a sigh. "Baby

Cakes, I appreciate your desire to be frugal, but I'm going to need you to tell me what you want to drink."

I let out my own sigh. "Fine, Mr. Kesso. If you want to spend a million dollars on breakfast, I'll have a peppermint mocha."

He nods. "Okay, then." And he's kind enough not to point out that the flavors I've named will clash.

"Order for Mikayla," someone farther down the bakery counter calls out, and my head automatically jerks in that direction.

A girl in her late teens rushes forward to take the white paper bag.

I relax.

It's not *the* Mikayla who just won the holiday *Second Bite*.

There was nothing wrong with her. She wasn't mean to me. But she was trying to flirt with Michael during the whole weekend, which was annoying. Though Michael did nothing to encourage her.

Then, the unwelcome image of Michael hugging Mikayla after she won flashes into my brain.

I turn my body toward Michael and glare up at him.

He keeps his arm on my shoulder, turning me into him even more.

"What's that Scrooge look for?" There's humor in his voice.

"I don't like you hugging other women." I keep my volume low, just for him.

Michael's brows raise, clearly not expecting me to say that. "I don't—"

"Mikayla," I whisper.

The corner of his mouth twitches. "That was for work, Baby. I didn't enjoy it."

"You better not have enjoyed it," I grumble.

His mouth tips up into even more of a smile. "It's just for work," he repeats.

"Fine." I straighten my stance as best I can. "But every time I see you hug another woman, I'm... I'm going to hug another man."

The smile drops off his face. "And who exactly would you hug?"

My mind races to think of an answer that will annoy him the most. "Joey," I blurt out, referencing the good-looking host of *Second Bite*.

Michael narrows his eyes and slides his hand from my shoulder to the back of my neck, holding me in place as he leans down so we're eye to eye. "It's Christmas Eve, Alice. Don't get on the naughty list now."

My pulse gallops through my veins.

His palm is so warm and large.

His presence even more so.

And every inch of my body is lighting up with the possibility of what my big chef would do to punish me.

His gaze drops to my mouth.

I catch my breath, forgetting all about the people around us. "Would you put coal in my stocking?"

Michael's exhale is rough. "I'll shove something in—"

"Next!" the cashier calls out, cutting off whatever Michael was about to say.

For the best, I'm sure.

My legs are a little shaky as we turn and step up to the counter.

The girl at the register is looking down as she says, "Welcome to Firm Buns, what can I get for..." She trails off, her mouth hanging open as she looks at Michael. "Chef... You're Chef M—"

I swear her face pales, and her hands start to shake.

"Morning." Michael nods to her.

"I-I..."

The poor girl can't seem to compose herself.

Then she looks at me.

I smile, trying to reassure her with friendliness.

The girl yelps.

Actually yelps, like she just got bit by a reindeer.

"Um, hello," I say awkwardly.

"Alice?" Her voice is higher pitched than it was before.

I lift my hand in a gesture that's supposed to be a wave, not sure how to act after getting recognized for the second time this morning.

I watch, stunned as her eyes fill with tears. "I love you."

My lips part. Then close.

Did this girl just say she loves me? Because of my three episodes on the show?

I answer the only way I can. "I love you too."

She sways.

Michael clears his throat next to me, and I glance up to see him trying not to smile.

How is he always so hot?

I turn my attention back to the girl and read her name off her apron. "Charise, would you like to sit down?"

She nods, then shakes her head. "No, no, I'm okay." Charise brushes a tear off her cheek. "You're so pretty."

A small laugh pops out of my chest at the unexpected compliment. "Thank you. You're pretty too."

Her face contorts, and she swipes at another tear. "You're just as nice as you seemed on the show." Charise's voice cracks. "And now you're..." She darts a look up at Michael. "You two were so cute on the show."

Feeling like it's the right thing to do, I reach across the counter and place my hand on her arm. "Thank you."

She sniffles, and one of her coworkers shouts out another completed order.

"Sorry. I've never met a famous person before." Charise lets out a strained laugh. "Never thought I'd be such a crier." She looks back up at Michael. "You're really great too, Chef Mike."

Michael grins. "Don't worry, I know she's my better half."

Charise sways again, and I start to really worry for her health.

"Is everything okay?" Another Firm Buns employee steps up beside Charise.

Charise waves her away. "I got it." Heaving out a breath, she nods once. "What can I get for you?"

I smile at her composure, but Michael answers before I can.

"One of your cranberry Danishes, two ham and cheese hand pies, a chocolate croissant, a peppermint mocha, a black coffee, and two bottles of water." He tips his head down to me. "Anything else?"

I resist rolling my eyes as I shake my head. "That should be enough."

Alice's hand trembles in mine.

"Baby Cakes," I say quietly as we walk together down the Jetway.

She jumps a little, making me frown.

The expression twists something inside me. "Are you okay?"

Her yes comes out high pitched and quick.

She's not okay.

Is she having doubts?

Am I moving this too fast?

I slow our steps and swallow. "If I'm rushing you—"

"Don't be ridiculous," Alice snaps, like she's mad I'd even think such a thing.

It's the exact reaction I need.

"Glad to hear that." I squeeze her fingers.

She huffs like she's still annoyed but continues on toward the plane.

Something is clearly still bothering her or making her nervous, but I can press her when we're in our seats.

It only takes a few seconds to catch up to the people in front of us. And together we stop just a few feet from the end of the Jetway, the interior of the plane in sight.

The line moves forward.

We step forward.

And just as I open my mouth to tell Alice to go on first, she halts.

She turns and looks up at me with wide eyes. "I've never done this before. I don't know what to do."

"Never done what before?"

Alice glances at the attendant waiting for us to board. "I've never flown."

My eyebrows rise in surprise, then I lower them in anger at myself for having assumed that flying was a normal experience.

"I'm okay." She hurries on to say. "I want to go. I just don't know..."

Softness for this woman fills my chest. "Do you want me to go first?"

She nods.

I move our joined hands behind my back. "Hold onto my belt."

Her fingers slip from mine, but then I feel them curling around the belt at my lower back.

I duck my head as we step onto the plane.

"Welcome aboard, Mr. Kesso." The attendant greets me with a wide smile.

I reply with a nod and turn down the aisle.

Alice squeaks out a hello to the attendant but keeps her hold on me.

I take two steps, then stop.

"This is us," I tell Alice over my shoulder.

Her hand drops away from my belt. "The first row?"

I turn enough so I can place my hand on her back and guide her in. "You take the window."

"You sure?"

"I'm sure, Sweetness."

She rolls her lips but doesn't argue and shuffles into the window seat.

Following, I lower into the seat beside hers.

This way she can look at the view and I can keep anyone from getting too close.

Chapter Seven

ALICE

I flatten my palms on my thighs in an effort to keep them from twisting in my skirt.

I wish I had my good-luck silver dollar in my pocket, but it's in my purse, which is wedged into the pocket on the wall in front of me. It's the one my grandma gave me, and the same one I lost in the hotel room a couple nights ago when Michael had his head up my skirt. Thankfully, Michael found it and returned it to my care just this morning. But since I was paranoid about losing it again, I decided to tuck it into my purse. However, now that we're minutes away from rocketing through the air, I'm tempted to retrieve it so I can have as much luck as possible.

Michael settles his hand over mine. "There's nothing to be nervous about."

I plaster on a smile as I turn to face him. "I'm okay."

His returning smile is soft. "You're still a bad liar."

A stressed chuckle pops out of my mouth. "And you're not supposed to point out my flaws."

Michael curls his fingers around mine. "It's hardly a flaw."

He lifts our joined hands and presses his lips to my wrist.

My pulse spikes, but this time it has nothing to do with the plane.

A throat clears, and I lift my eyes to find the attendant grinning down at us. "Can I get you two something to drink before we take off?"

Before we take off? That's a thing?

I glance at the mini water bottles that were left on the armrest between Michael and myself.

I want to ask if these are for us and if they're free, but I also don't want to sound like a bumpkin that doesn't belong in first class, let alone on a plane.

"Maybe some ginger ale?" Michael suggests, and my love for him grows even more.

"Ginger ale would be nice."

After the attendant steps away, I squeeze Michael's hand. "Thank you for that."

He dips his chin. "You can thank me by never talking about touching Joey ever again."

I stare at Michael for a moment. "What?"

He leans in closer. "You're little threat earlier, about hugging Joey." He lifts a brow like he's daring me to argue. "You're not to go near him."

I lift my brow in response. "Are you going to stop hugging the winners?"

He stares at me a beat before he nods. "You'll be the only person I hug from here until forever."

I know it's a ridiculous request for me to make. I know it's for his job. But I still nod. "It's a deal."

Chapter Eight

MICHAEL

As the plane starts to pull away from the terminal, Alice tenses beside me.

She's holding my hand in both of hers on her lap, squeezing my fingers like I might disappear.

I need to distract her.

"So." I stretch my legs out. "When did you first become obsessed with me?"

Her quiet gasp is adorable.

I flex my fingers on her thigh. "I saw that box, remember?"

Slowly, I turn my head toward her.

Her cheeks are turning the cutest shade of pink.

"I should've made you pack it," I say, thinking out loud.

The second I laid eyes on Alice, I knew I had to have her. So discovering her little box, the one filled with news clippings and photographs of me, was a huge relief.

I'd been worried my instant need would scare her away, but if she was already obsessing over me, then it's just proof we're meant to be.

"I'm not obsessed with you." She huffs. "I'm in love with you. There's a difference."

I snort. "Not between us, Sugar Cookie. Our love is obsession, and that's okay."

She finally looks up at me. "I think I kinda like that."

I feel the plane shift direction, but Alice doesn't seem to notice. "So what was it? What did I do to catch your attention?" The way she squirms makes me smirk. "If just thinking about it makes you react like that, then you have to tell me."

Alice blows out a breath. "It was season one, episode three."

I'm sure my grin looks as wide as a nutcracker's, but I can't help it.

Alice sees my expression and rolls her eyes.

"And what in particular caught your attention that episode?" I remember all the contestants I've met, but I can't always keep track of what happened when.

Alice heaves out a breath. "You were eating a frosted donut and got some of the buttercream on the side of your mouth."

And just like that, I know exactly what she's talking about.

The innocent moment when I used my thumb to swipe the frosting off the side of my mouth and then licked it off has been spread around the internet in GIF and meme form. It was a good lesson, and I've learned to use napkins.

"I already thought you were handsome." Alice carries on. "But that moment... did something to me."

The tone of her voice is doing something to me too. And for the first time ever, I'm glad I did what I did.

She traces her fingertip across the back of my hand. "I tried not to be a freak about it, but the more I watched the show, the more I couldn't stop thinking about you. And then—"

The plane picks up speed.

"And then what?" I prompt.

Alice grips my hand but keeps her focus on me. "Then I read an article about a visit you made to a high school." Her eyes are shining now. "All those scholarships you gave out... That was really great of you."

"It was nothing."

She shakes her head. "No, Chef Michael, it was everything."

Then, with her focus on me, the nose of the plane tilts up, and we take off.

Chapter Nine

ALICE

My body jostles, and my eyes drift open.

It takes me a second to remember that I'm on an airplane and that apparently I slept through my first flight.

I blink at the gray light coming in through the window next to me. I know Canada has a lot of wilderness, but this seems like a lot.

I lean closer to the window.

I don't actually know what the Vancouver airport looks like. But I've seen enough Canadian home renovation shows to know it's a metropolis. And this...

I look out the window at the handful of single-story airplane hangars and evergreen trees as far as the eye can see.

· This looks like the middle of nowhere.

"Um, Michael." I keep staring outside.

"I didn't want to wake you up and alarm you."

"Alarm me?" I turn away from the window to look at Michael.

"We—"

The overhead speakers crackle to life. "Thanks for bearing with us through this diversion. We've landed safely in Bear Cove and have been told a few hotels in the vicinity should be able to house everyone for the next couple of nights. When the flight attendants give you the all clear to unbuckle and deboard the plane, please follow the signs to baggage claim, and airport staff will be ready to help you with your bookings. Welcome to Canada, and happy Christmas Eve."

The pilot's words bounce around in my half-asleep head as I try to make sense of it all.

"Why were we diverted?" I whisper.

"Blizzard," Michael answers.

I look back out the window.

There is no precipitation falling, but the sky is a solid gray. A sure sign of snow.

"A couple of nights?" I repeat what the pilot said.

As a Minnesotan, I'm used to big snowstorms. But I've never been stuck away from home during one.

Michael pulls his phone out of his pocket and checks the screen. "According to the radar, we have about an hour before the snow will start. And my manager just got back to me. He has a place for us."

Chapter Ten

ALICE

I can't stop myself from leaning forward as Michael drives up the tree-lined driveway.

From Michael's tone when he was on the phone with his manager earlier, I got the impression he doesn't care for the man much. But right now, the adorable Christmas cottage in front of me is nearly enough to have me breaking our new *no hugging others* rule.

"Hoppin' holidays, this place is perfect."

Michael makes a sound in his throat. "Better than crammed into one of those motels with everyone else."

"Also true, but seriously, what is this place?"

Michael pulls the Jeep—that was somehow waiting for us at the little airport—to a stop in front of the cottage.

It's one story, with a literal picket fence sticking out of the snow covering the front yard. The entire roofline is trimmed with multicolored Christmas lights, and a lit tree is visible through the large picture window.

"Some rental my manager tracked down." Michael turns off the engine. "Apparently people were supposed to be checking in tonight to spend the holiday here, but their flight never left the ground, so we were able to take over their reservation."

"It's so pretty." I feel my eyes turn into little hearts as big, fluffy snowflakes start to fall from the sky.

Before we left the airport, Michael wisely made me dig my winter jacket out of my luggage. And as I follow Michael out of the vehicle, I zip it up to brace against the cold.

Meeting Michael at the back of the Jeep, I reach for my suitcase, but he gently pushes my hand down and pulls it out himself.

Only after I insist does Michael let me help with the bags of groceries.

Across the street from the airport was the local Bear Cove mini-mart. Michael offered to let me stay in the car, but with a sign that read *We've Got Jerky from Elk to Turkey*, I had to go in and experience it for myself.

The selection was surprisingly good, and I'm sure we purchased too much, but considering we're about to spend Christmas holed up inside, it's probably better to be safe than sorry.

Chapter Eleven

MICHAEL

I can't keep my eyes off Alice as we step inside the cottage.

She points at everything—the tree, the garland-trimmed window, the red and green blankets and pillows decoratively strewn across the living room furniture.

I set the suitcases down at the end of the little hallway that must lead to the bedroom and take the grocery bags from her.

Alice lets out a sound of excitement when we step into the kitchen.

The house itself is small, just one bedroom and bathroom, but the living room on the front side of the house is spacious and the kitchen overlooking the backyard is just as large.

There's a marble-topped island with stools on the far side and a little breakfast nook in front of the windows.

"Oh, look!" Alice rushes to the patio doors, lifting her hands like she's going to place them on the glass but lowering them before they make contact. "There's a hot tub."

I place the bags on the island and move to stand next to her. "Good thing it's on the back of the house."

She tips her head back. "Why?"

I settle my hand on her perfect ass. "Because we didn't pack swimsuits."

Chapter Twelve

ALICE

I pause when I step barefoot into the surprisingly modern bathroom.

Are these floors heated?

I wiggle my toes.

Good lord, the floors are heated.

Sighing, I pull open the glass door leading into the large walk-in shower and reach in to start the water.

I've heard people talk about how they feel kind of gross after flying, and now that I've finally done it, I get what they mean.

When I mentioned wanting to wash my face, Michael told me to just take a shower and put on my pajamas while he put away the food and made us a snack.

It's hardly late enough to go to bed, but it's not like we're going anywhere, so why not start my slumber party with Michael now?

With my discarded dress on the floor and my pajamas on the counter, I test the warmth of the water, then step into the spray.

Standing under the lush stream, I close my eyes and take the moment to appreciate how much my life has changed in a matter of days.

This time last week, I was newly unemployed and moving out of my little apartment and into my cousins' unfinished basement.

I was still content with my life. And at that point, the knowledge that I was going to be a contestant on *Second Bite*—that I'd meet Chef Mike Kesso in person—that bit of joy would have been enough to get me through another thirty years.

But then our eyes met. And his attention was electric. And the pull I felt for him went from fantasy to reality.

I take a small step back, tipping my head away so the stream can hit my breasts.

When Michael came to my hotel room and our lips met for the first time, I finally knew what lust was.

Finally understood.

My pulse starts to speed at the memory.

And then my memory takes me to last night, when Michael walked down those stairs into my makeshift bedroom... that lust turned into an inferno.

I set my palms on my sides, wondering if it's wrong to touch myself thinking about Michael when he's just down the hall.

My hands slide a bit higher.

I shouldn't.

Before I can drop them, large hands clamp over mine.

"Do it, Sweetie." Michael's voice vibrates through my body and straight to the juncture between my legs. "Squeeze those big tits for me. Show me how you like it."

His large naked body presses into my back, and I feel his hard cock hot and solid against the top of my ass.

Doing as he says, I slide my hands up until they're cupping my breasts.

I've never showered with a man before. Never stood naked under this much light with a man before. But I won't let self-consciousness ruin this for me. Not with the way his body is reacting to mine.

I squeeze my breasts together, pushing them up, causing the water to cascade down my cleavage.

Michael groans and stretches his fingers past mine to pluck at my nipples.

The sensation has me arching my back, pushing my ass against his dick.

"Michael," I breathe.

He applies more pressure to my nipples. "You like that, Baby?"

I nod.

"How much do you like it?" Michael rolls my nipples between his fingers.

"So much," I pant.

"Enough to get that sugar-sweet pussy wet for me?"

It's my turn to groan, his dirty mouth doing just as much to me as his fingers.

He pinches my nipples harder. "Answer me, Alice." He rocks his hips into me. "Or do I need to check for myself?"

"I... What?" The stimulation is too much, and I can't focus on the questions he's asking me.

Michael chuckles next to my ear. "My perfect little Christmas angel, so lit up she can't even think straight."

One of his hands drops away, and I lower one of mine to catch it.

I want more.

I need more.

But when I catch his wrist, it doesn't stop him.

Michael flattens his hand on my belly but doesn't pause as he slides it lower.

"So soft." Past my belly button. "So beautiful." Down the rounded part below. "So feminine." Into the blonde curls, right above the place I want his touch most.

"Please." I dig my fingers into his wrist, wanting to feel the muscles beneath his skin shift as he touches me.

"Please, what?"

His touch is nearly there.

"Please, I need you."

Lips close around my earlobe at the same time his hand shifts and his fingers slip into me.

Chapter Thirteen

MICHAEL

Her wet heat practically pulls me in.

I clamp my teeth onto the bottom of Alice's ear, causing her to tremble.

"Holy..." Alice lets go of my wrist and slaps her hands against the shower wall in front of her.

My chuckle is strained because as much as I love seeing her fall apart, I'm right there with her.

I release her nipple and hook my arm around her waist, steadying her as I slide my middle finger deeper into her slit.

Her slickness coats my hand even as the water streams around us.

I pump my finger inside her. "I want to spin you around and kiss you." I add a second finger. "But I also want to fuck you just like this. With my hips slamming against your ass."

She groans and wiggles against my fingers.

I press my open mouth to her shoulder and breathe her in.

"Or maybe." I slide my fingers out, adding a third, teasing her entrance but not pushing in. "Maybe I should let you control how deep I go."

Keeping the tips of my fingers stretching her core, I use my other arm to pull her with me as I back up.

There's a stool in the corner that was probably put there for decoration as much as function, but it looks sturdy enough for my needs.

Alice's hands fall away from the wall, and as she shuffles backward, her inner muscles tense, trying to drag me in.

The backs of my knees bump into the stool, and I lower myself until I'm sitting on the edge, knees spread.

"One more step back," I tell Alice as I move my hands so I'm gripping her hips.

She glances over her shoulder at me. "Shouldn't I turn around?"

"No, Baby Cakes." I shake my head and let go of her with one hand to grip the base of my cock. "You're gonna stay facing that way so you can sit on my dick."

I hear her breath hitch over the sound of the shower.

My dick throbs as I give it one firm stroke.

"I've never..."

"Goddamn right, you've never." I flex my fingers into the soft flesh of her hip. "Now, be a good little girl and sit on my lap. Tell me what you want most for Christmas."

"M-Michael."

I pull her down. "Oh, you'll get me, Alice. Every day of the year."

As she lowers her hips, she reaches down to grab my thighs.

I keep my grip on my dick, lining it up where it needs to go.

"That's it, Baby. Just sit down." I urge.

"I don't think I can," she whimpers.

"You can do anything." I encourage her.

I need this.

I need her to be the one to sink onto me.

I need to know, like really know, that she wants this as badly as I do.

Alice lowers another inch, and the tip of my cock bumps into her slit.

She's so slippery, so wet and warm, I let out a moan.

"Oh, oh god." Alice grips my thighs harder.

"That's it." I let go of my dick, my tip lodged in her pussy, and raise my hand back to her hip. "Just take what you want. You're in control."

Her inner muscles flex around me, and I hiss.

"Michael." She turns her head to look back at me. "I want it all."

I open my mouth to reply, but then Alice drops her hips down until she's settled against my lap, sinking my whole length inside her.

Chapter Fourteen

ALICE

My head falls forward, and I fight to breathe.

Michael's cock is so big it's almost a struggle to fit him.

I took him last night, but standing like this, with my muscles clenched to stay upright, he feels different. Bigger. Snugger.

Michael's groan is so loud it echoes around the shower stall.

Pride fills me.

I'm doing this.

I'm the one causing Michael to make those sounds.

I lift my hips a few inches, arching my back as I do so I can keep a hold of Michael's legs.

I'm so slick, the motion is smooth.

"Alice." Michael doesn't loosen his grip on my hips.

I lower back down, and we both groan.

Up and down again.

I'm overstimulated.

Up and down.

Every inch of me is needy. Ready.

Up and down.

My legs start to tremble.

Up and down.

The feeling of being so full is making it hard to keep my balance.

Up and down.

"I'm not gonna last," I pant out as I wiggle all the way down again.

"Me either." Michael's voice is gruff.

I'd been referring to my legs, but hearing Michael sound so close to the edge takes me right there with him.

The fingers on my hip move, sliding around to my front. Sliding down to the spot straining for attention.

"Don't come until I do," Michael demands as he strokes my clit. "Lift those hips again." He touches where we're connected, gathering more wetness. "Just a few more times."

I do as he says, straightening my legs, flexing my muscles, lifting off him.

Up and down.

Each time is just as intense as the last.

Up and down.

Each time feels just as new.

Up and down.

His fingers start rubbing circles as his cock drags against something inside me.

My core clenches.

"Once more." His words are ragged, and I swear I can feel his dick getting thicker. "One more time, Baby."

Up.

I rise until it feels like he's almost all the way out.

My thighs shake.

My lungs struggle to take in air.

And this time when Michael brushes over my clit, I implode.

Chapter Fifteen

MICHAEL

All at once, Alice flies off the edge.

Her body tenses.

Her pussy pulses around my tip.

And her head flies back with a loud moan.

I wrap my arm around her, my other hand still playing with her little clit, and I move my knees closer together before I jerk her back down.

She cries out as she sits firmly onto my lap, her body spasming around my length as I bury myself to the hilt.

And that's all it takes.

My body follows hers, as it will until the end of time, and I empty myself inside her.

Chapter Sixteen

ALICE

I give up on my seated position, having eaten my fill, and scoot down the mattress. "That was the perfect amount."

Michael grunts, setting the serving tray on his nightstand. "If you get hungry later, you can dip into Santa's share."

I lift my head to see the four chocolate-covered pretzels, three green grapes, two broken crackers, and the one strawberry left on the plate.

"Such a bounty." I snicker and drop my head back down.

After our shower, when I regained use of my legs, we stuck with the original plan of pajamas and snacks—only the snacks were in bed.

"All the cookies and milk, I'm sure he'll enjoy the change up."

"Uh-huh, sure." I roll onto my side so I'm facing Michael. "If you want to stay up..." I let my offer linger, hoping he doesn't take me up on it.

He shakes his head and shifts so he's lying down facing me. "It's been a busy few days for both of us, so we might as well catch up on some sleep while we can."

I place my hand against his bare chest, enjoying the fact that his pajamas consist only of boxer briefs. "Thank you for bringing me on this trip."

Michael gives his head a little shake. "There's nothing to thank me for, as you didn't really have an option to say no."

I smile. "I still can't believe this is real. I've lain in bed so many nights thinking of you. Imagining what you'd be like."

It feels weird to admit that to the man himself, the one whose photo sat on my bedside table for years. But his look of smug adoration lets me know that telling him was the right thing to do.

"I can hardly believe it either, future Mrs. Kesso. But it is real. So damn real."

And then he proves his words by pressing his lips to mine.

Chapter Seventeen

MICHAEL

When her breath evens out, I reach behind me and turn off the light on the nightstand.

Darkness settles across the room, but we left the curtains open, allowing in the glow of the outdoor Christmas lights and the moon's reflection off the falling snow.

I watch the puffy flakes as they fall on the other side of the glass and decide this is my new favorite holiday.

Carefully, I pull Alice against my chest and wrap my arms around her.

Life gave me the most precious gift, and here, tonight, I vow to take care of her in every way I can.

Chapter Eighteen

ALICE

Sweet scents pull me out of sleep, and it's the most pleasant way I've ever woken up.

I stretch out, finding Michael's side of the bed warm but empty.

Michael.

I smile as I blink my eyes open.

It's Christmas morning, quite possibly my favorite day of the year, and I get to spend it with Michael Kesso.

Then I blink my eyes again.

The sight beyond the open curtains is nothing short of breathtaking.

I sit up and turn toward the view.

The backyard is small, surrounded by towering evergreens, and every inch of it is covered in snow.

Lots of snow.

And it's still falling.

The floor quietly creaks as I cross to the window, and my smile turns into a grin when I see that not every inch is covered.

A path has been shoveled to the hot tub, proving that Michael has been busy this morning.

No swimsuits and a hot tub in the snow. Merry Christmas to me.

Not wanting to miss a moment of today, I rush through my routine in the bathroom, emerging with freshly brushed teeth and my hair up in a frizzy bun. I'm still in my pajamas, a super short sleep dress with thin straps and a low-cut front—courtesy of my cousins, who slipped it into my suitcase with a Post-it that said *wear me*.

I don't know if they had already gotten it for me as a gift or if it belonged to one of them already, but if ever there was a day to wear something provocative...

And if I get cold in this skimpy outfit, I'm sure I can convince Michael to warm me up.

Following my nose, I pad down the short hall into the kitchen. And then I stop.

Before me, in the flesh, is Michael, *in the flesh*.

Literally.

His back is to me, and I can't stop staring at his ass. His *clad only in bright red boxer briefs* ass.

It's an ass I'd write to Santa for, if it wasn't already mine.

I step closer, smug satisfaction filling every inch of me.

"Looks delicious," I say in greeting.

Michael glances at me over his shoulder, smirk already in place. "Merry Christmas." His eyes travel up and down my body. "My little snow elf."

Then he turns the rest of the way to face me, and, jingle my bells, I have to swallow.

I've never seen a hotter image in my life.

Michael has put on a green apron that covers his boxer briefs, making him look naked. In an apron. In a kitchen that smells like heaven.

"Everything okay?" His tone is knowing, even as he stares at my chest.

I step forward and dip my fingers into the open bag of flour on the counter.

"I'm sorry," I say, then I gently slap my hand on his bare shoulder.

Michael lowers his gaze to the dusty print on his skin, then looks back up at me. "You don't seem very sorry."

I grin. "I'm not. You just looked too perfect."

"And now?" He raises a brow.

I purse my lips as I consider, then I dip my fingers back in the flour. "Still too perfect."

He lets my hand connect with his other shoulder, then he snags my wrist and pulls me to him. "Naughty girl."

I'm laughing when our lips connect, but Michael quickly swallows that laughter.

Chocolate and spices swirl around us as Michael deepens the kiss.

He slides his hands around my sides to my back, holding me close.

I lean into him and drag my own hands up his back, enjoying the feel of his muscles flexing under my touch.

His lips part and I slide my tongue across his, eliciting a groan from deep in his throat.

Michael lets me taste him, for one more heartbeat, before he pulls away.

"That's enough of that, Sweetness." He takes a step back. "I promised myself I'd feed you before I fucked you again."

I cross my arms. "What a grinch."

"Go sit down." He reaches for the whisk sitting on the counter, and I jump out of the way before he can pretend to swat me with it.

After circling around the island, I pull out one of the stools and settle in to watch him work.

"What are you making?" I ask.

He turns back to the stove. "Raspberry pancakes."

"Ooo."

"With a white chocolate sauce."

"Well, stuff my stocking, that sounds amazing."

Michael chuckles.

"Is that your usual Christmas morning food?" I ask as my mouth starts watering.

Michael shakes his head. "Can't say I have a usual. Normally, I'm on the road filming for the holidays."

I drum my fingers against the counter. "Technically, you are this year too."

He turns and sets a steaming mug in front of me. "This year is different."

I lift the milky drink and inhale the rich coffee steam. "Different good, right?"

"Different perfect. Though you should hardly have to ask."

Michael turns back to the stove, hovering his hand above the large flat griddle on top of the burners, checking to see if it's ready for the batter, while I go back to staring at his ass.

He reaches for the bowl of batter to his right. "Now tell me about baking with your grandmother."

I blink.

Something about admiring someone's butt cheeks while they mention your deceased relative feels a little weird.

I clear my throat. "Um..."

"You were supposed to tell me about her on the plane." He glances back at me. "But you decided to sleep instead."

I snort. "I still can't believe I did that."

Then, after taking a sip of coffee, I tell him.

I tell Michael about my grandma. How she always had these little *silver dollar chocolate chip cookies* in her freezer. How she gave me the actual silver dollar as a token of luck—and to remind me of her. How she passed her love for baking on to me.

I tell him about Christmas Eves always spent at her house. How we'd eat until we couldn't eat anymore. How the focus was always on the feast and how presents were the last thing we cared about.

"The little candle chime thing was always my favorite part of the table setting." I sigh. "I don't know what happened to it."

Michael slides another trio of pancakes into the warm oven. "The what?"

"It's a... I don't know how to describe it." I look around and spot a notebook on one of the counters. I slide off the stool and collect it, then go back to my seat. "I'm not very good at drawing." I state the obvious as I start to sketch. "I think maybe it was made of brass, but it was shiny gold and kinda looked like a skinny carousel. It had candles circling the bottom and a trio of angels on the top part. And when you lit the candles, the heat made the angels go around in a circle, causing them to chime bells on every turn." I bite my lip as I frown at my drawing. "I'm doing a terrible job describing this."

I startle when Michael's heat presses against my back.

He reaches past me to pull the notebook to the side so he can see it. "You're a better artist than you give yourself credit for."

I sigh. "And you're being kind."

Michael kisses the top of my head. "We'll find one of these chime things before next Christmas."

Next Christmas.

The sigh I let out this time is different.

Contented.

And as Michael walks back around the island, his glutes looking like holiday hams in those boxer briefs, I wonder again how I got so damn lucky.

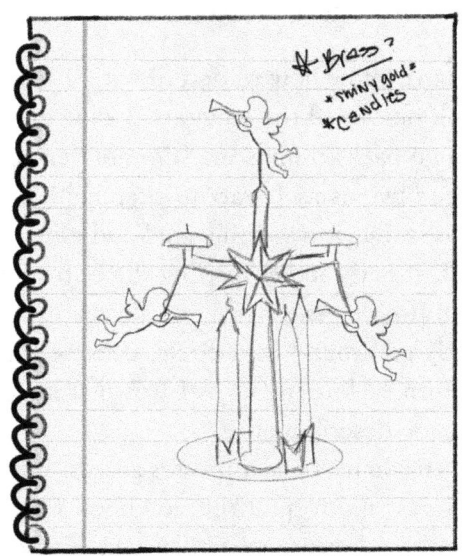

Chapter Nineteen

MICHAEL

Alice tips her head back as she moans around another mouthful of pancake, and I can't fucking take it anymore.

My dick has been half-hard since she walked into the kitchen in that slutty little dress. And it's been fully hard since she took her first bite.

"It's so good," she breathes.

And seriously, I can't wait anymore.

I never was one for delayed gratification.

Reaching behind myself, I undo the tie of my apron, then pull the fabric up over my head.

Alice finally lifts her gaze from her plate to look at me. "What are—"

I grip my cock through the thin layer of cotton as I plant my feet on the floor and push my chair back from the table. "Come here."

Her mouth drops partially open. Her eyes on my hand as I stroke myself through the fabric. And I can see the change, the hitch in her breathing, the lowering of her eyelids.

In the blink of an eye, she goes from focused on food to a horny little vixen.

"Such a responsive girl." I pull the top band of my boxer briefs down, letting just the head of my cock stick out.

"Michael," she whispers, shifting in her seat.

My eyes lower to her tits, and her nipples are straining against the fabric in a way they weren't just a moment ago. "Two seconds of watching, and your body is already priming itself for me."

Her lips move, but this time no sound comes out.

"Now come over here, Baby Cakes." I lift my hips and shove my boxer briefs down until my whole length is exposed. "And sit on Santa's dick."

Alice's fork clatters against her plate as she stands.

I lift my free hand to halt her. "Bring the sauce."

Her eyes are wide, but she doesn't argue.

Alice slides the mini carafe half-full of chocolate sauce across the table so it's next to my plate.

"Good girl." I praise her, then I pat my lap.

She takes two steps toward me, then pauses.

I narrow my eyes, but before I can question her, Alice reaches up under her skirt.

Keeping her eyes on me, she slides her panties down her legs, letting them pool around her ankles.

She steps out of them, and my heart jumps in reply.

Perfection.

Another step, and she's within reach.

I grip her hips and pull her in until she's standing next to my chair, her green eyes shining as they gaze into mine.

"Is it my turn to sit here, Mr. Santa?" Alice bats her lashes.

My dick bobs in reply.

I've never role-played before.

Never once thought of it.

But fuck me, I'm into it.

I tighten my fingers on her hips. "Climb on, Sweetie, and tell me if you've been good."

Alice reaches down and grips my cock.

My eyes start to close at her touch, but I force them back open.

I'm not missing a second of this.

"That's the thing," Alice whispers as she lifts her leg over my lap, "I don't think I've been very good." She points my dick at her entrance, balancing herself with her other hand on my shoulder.

My lungs struggle to fill. "What have you been, Little Alice?"

Her mouth pulls up on one side in a devious smile. "I've been bad. Very bad."

Then she drops down, and my cock is swallowed by her heat.

"Fuck." I half groan, half shout as her bare ass connects with my thighs, her pussy surrounding every inch of my dick.

The sneaky look that had been on her face is replaced by one of shocked ecstasy.

She impaled herself on my dick, and now she's reaping the consequences.

I dig my fingers into her sides, holding her where she is, keeping her snug on my lap, as her muscles flutter around me.

"So bad," I groan.

She nods. "So, so bad."

The morning sun is streaming in through the window behind me, illuminating her like some sort of magical winter sprite.

Her golden hair is practically glowing, and I let go of her hip and pull her hair free from the bun she'd tied it up in.

The messy curls drop around her shoulders, and I flex my hips, forcing my cock just a bit deeper.

"You know what happens to bad girls?" I growl.

Alice shakes her head, her curls bouncing with the motion.

"They have to do as they're told." I stretch my arm out and hook the handle for the sauce. "And I'm telling you to sit very still."

My voice is scratchier than normal. Rough. And I know this is going to be as torturous for me as it will be for her.

Alice grips my shoulders. "I'll try my best."

But even as she says it, her pussy contracts around me.

I click my tongue. "So naughty." Then I yank down the front of her dress.

Chapter Twenty

ALICE

My breasts spill free, my already hard nipples pebbling further as they're exposed to the cool air.

"So delicious," Michael says.

And then something warm is running down my chest, and I can't sit still anymore.

The white chocolate sauce runs down Alice's chest, trailing a line down one of her big, glorious tits.

It's graphic.

Vulgar.

And enough to send a pulse of release seeping out of my dick.

Then she starts to squirm.

Every movement she makes squeezes around my already straining cock.

Her tits bounce, and I wait until the perfect moment, wait until the sauce makes its way to where I want it before I tell her what to do next.

Chapter Twenty-Two

ALICE

"Feed it to me," Michael demands.

The creamy sauce has dripped down to my nipple, and nothing in this world could stop me from doing what Michael says.

I let go of his shoulder and grip my breast, lifting it, holding it up, so he can—

Michael flattens his tongue against my nipple and licks.

He licks and licks.

He leans closer and licks up my breast, lapping up the line of chocolate.

He moans and groans, and when he works his way back down, he sucks my nipple into his mouth.

I can't take it anymore.

I keep doing what he asked, I keep feeding him, keep my grip on my tit. But I also move my other hand down and reach under the skirt of my dress.

Chapter Twenty-Three

MICHAEL

I feel her fingers between us. Feel them moving. Rubbing at her clit.

I drag my teeth over her sensitive skin. "Such a bad girl. Touching herself without permission."

"I'm sorry," Alice cries, but she doesn't stop. "I'm sorry. I have to."

Instead of pouring the sauce, this time, I dip two fingers into the dish.

I swipe the chocolate across her other nipple.

"You have to what?" I ask, working to sound unaffected while accepting that I'm punishing myself with this more than I'm punishing her.

"I need to come." Her movements are getting more frantic. "Please, Santa. Please let me come."

My cock throbs.

"Suck my fingers clean." I lift my chocolate-smeared fingers to her mouth. "Suck them clean, and you can come, Little Alice."

I close my lips around her nipple and push my fingers into her mouth.

She sucks on them like they're made of candy, her tongue swirling around, drawing off every speck of sweetness.

She's trembling.

Moaning.

Sucking and rocking.

And then she's exploding.

Her mouth opens, and my fingers press against her tongue as she arches her back and comes all over my cock.

I can't sit still anymore.

Wrapping my arms around her, I stand.

Chapter Twenty-Four

ALICE

My world tips.

Stars are still bursting behind my eyes, and I hear something scrape across the table, then I'm on it.

My back connects with the solid wood of the breakfast table, and my legs hitch up, my heels digging into Michael's back.

I think I might be chanting something.

Maybe his name.

Maybe a prayer.

My body is still thrumming.

And then Michael starts to fuck me.

Chapter Twenty-Five

MICHAEL

I snap my hips forward, slamming my full length deep into Alice's sweet pussy.

I thrust again and again.

The plates rattle. Coffee sloshes out of the mugs onto the table. And I keep going.

I can't stop.

This is my woman.

My woman, who just climbed onto my lap.

My woman, who let me lick chocolate off her tits.

My woman, who sucked on my fingers as if they were my cock.

My woman, who just came all over my fucking lap.

And I need to claim her.

I need to mark her.

I need every inch of her to understand that she's mine.

Alice reaches for me, and I lower myself over her.

I don't stop moving.

Don't stop sliding in and out of her heat.

She wraps her arms around my neck and pulls my ear to her mouth.

"I've been so bad," she whimpers.

My balls tighten.

"Teach me a lesson and fill me full," she pleads.

I slam my hips forward one last time, then I do exactly as she said, and I fill her to the brim with my Christmas cream.

Chapter Twenty-Six

ALICE

Michael hangs up his phone. "I have bad news."

I lift my head from his lap to look back at him. "What is it?"

He strokes a hand down my hair. "Our flight out is tomorrow."

I bite down on a smile. "That's bad news?"

Michael nods. "I was hoping for another week or two here."

My grin breaks through. "Maybe we can rent it out again." Then my grin falters when I remember how absolutely broke I am.

Michael pulls on my shoulder, rolling me onto my back, and glides his thumb across my lower lip. "What's that sudden frown for?"

I heave out a breath and try to sit up, but Michael places his hand on my chest, holding me in place.

"I want to help..." I wonder if there's a delicate way to talk about this.

He tips his head. "Help with what?"

I lift my hands and let them drop onto my stomach. "With renting this place. Or buying groceries. Or plane tickets..."

Michael shakes his head. "You don't have to do any of those things."

"I—" I can't say this lying down.

Twisting my fingers with Michael's, I pull his hand to the side so I can sit up.

He lets me this time, but when I turn to face him, he grabs my free hand with his so we're as entwined as possible.

"I moved into my cousins' place because the company I'd been working for... closed." I let my cheeks puff out on an exhale. "I don't even know if it was bankruptcy or what, but my last handful of paychecks bounced, and I've accepted that I'll never get that money."

"Baby—" Michael starts, but I squeeze his hands.

"I'm not telling you as some sort of sob story. I just want you to know. And I want you to know I'm not interested in your money." His lips pull up into the softest smile. "I only want you, Michael. And I don't expect you to just start paying for my life. Okay?"

He dips his chin. "Anything else?"

I shrug. "I have a little bit of credit card debt, but even with low-income scholarships, I couldn't afford to go to college, so at least I don't have student loans." When Michael starts to frown, I flex my fingers in his again. "That's a good thing. And learning from you will be better than any college class."

He sighs. "First, I'll teach you anything you want to know, but you've proven yourself to be an accomplished baker already." He closes one eye. "Just not so skilled with Jell-O."

My mouth drops open. "Too soon."

Michael's lips twitch.

I can't believe he brought that up, but it did take that hint of sadness off his features, so I guess it's okay.

"Second." He continues. "If you want to take classes, we'll make it happen." I open my mouth to retort, but it's his turn to squeeze my fingers. "Third, you're mine. And I take care of what's mine. I know you're not after my money. And I appreciate that. But you're the love of my life, Alice, and I'm going to use my considerable fortune to spoil you until the day I die. Even if you had money, I wouldn't let you spend it."

"Michael—"

"Fourth, fifth, whatever number we're on." He talks over me. "If you want to work, we'll find something for you to do. But only if you really want to."

I chew on my cheek. "Like what?"

"Anything." He thinks for a second. "Maybe something with scholarships."

A lightness fills my chest. "Really?"

Michael nods. "Yeah. I've supported a lot of causes, but I've never started one on my own. We could have our own foundation that sponsors culinary students. Do fundraisers, whatever."

My poor heart thuds inside my ribs. "You mean it, don't you? You'd really do it?"

He lifts his brows. "What? Like it's hard?"

I narrow my eyes at the older man before me. "Did you really just quote the movie I think you did?"

"No idea what you're talking about, Baby Cakes."

I keep my eyes narrowed for another moment, then use my hold on his hands to pull myself forward until my weight shifts to my knees and I can throw my arms around his neck. "Thank you, my Chef. I love you."

Warm lips press against the side of my neck. "I love you too." A beeping sounds from the kitchen. "Now give me a kiss before our dinner burns."

Chapter Twenty-Seven

MICHAEL

"Aha!" Alice shouts in triumph from down the hall.

I finish drying the pot in my hands and set it down on the counter. "What's going on back there?"

"One sec!" Her words are followed by muttering I can't make out.

Attempting to be patient, I move my attention to opening the bottle of local Bear Cove wine I bought at the mart.

Patience is hard around Alice since I want to have my hands on her every damn second.

I know we've only been together a couple days, but I don't think this feeling is ever going to fade. This need for nearness that I have.

But I'm trying to control myself.

For instance, I sat through our entire dinner without putting my dick in her.

Bravo for me.

I pour two glasses of the deep red liquid, then bring one to my nose.

Impressed by the smell, I'm taking a sip when Alice steps into the kitchen, clutching a fluffy white robe around her body.

"They're made for skinny people." She sticks a leg forward,

causing the robe to part around her upper thigh, demonstrating that the opposing sides of the robe are barely touching. "But they'll do."

I take another sip of wine. "What are you wearing under there?"

Alice bites her lip, then she quickly pulls the robe open, then shut, showing me exactly what she's wearing underneath the robe.

Which is nothing.

My blood heats, and I tip the wine glass back, swallowing the rest of it in two gulps.

Alice laughs. "What are you doing?"

"Fortifying my patience."

She wraps an arm around herself, holding the robe in place, and reaches for the second glass on the counter. "Is it working?"

I shake my head and step toward her.

She takes a step back, aiming toward the sliding glass door that leads from the kitchen to the patio. "Your robe is on the bed."

"Is that so?" I take another step.

She matches it with her retreat.

She takes another quick step toward the door. "Bring the bottle when you come out."

Chapter Twenty-Eight

ALICE

Steam dances up from the surface of the hot tub, and I sink down farther until the water is lapping at my chin.

Michael came out before dinner to make sure the temperature would be perfect, and with the glow of the moon and the twinkle of the Christmas lights... perfect it is.

The snow stopped falling this afternoon, and by evening, the roads—and our little driveway—were plowed.

I'm excited for Vancouver. Excited to travel more. To see the set for the New Year's special Michael has to record. But I'm equally excited to spend the rest of this evening with Michael—alone. Out here, surrounded by towering snow-covered evergreens.

The sound of the patio door opening has me sitting up.

Michael is gripping his robe closed with one hand, and in the other is his glass and the bottle of wine.

"Hi." I greet him shyly.

He stops at the edge of the hot tub and sets the glass and wine down on the flat rim.

"Hi, Baby." His tone is casual as he releases his grip on his robe, revealing his hard cock.

I choke on nothing. The winter air crystalizing in my lungs.

Michael shrugs out of his robe and drapes it over the deck railing next to mine.

It shouldn't come as a surprise, his nakedness. He's wearing exactly as much as I am. But, for some reason, I hadn't expected him to walk out hard.

He curls his fingers around the base of his dick. "Watch your wine, Sweetness."

"Huh?" I look up at his face, then register what he said and look down at the glass in my hand.

A few drops of wine drip over the rim of my tilted glass, disappearing into the churning water below.

"Oops." I right the glass as I return my gaze to Michael's cock.

I can't take my eyes off it.

Can't stop staring at the thick vein running the length of it.

Can't stop my mouth from watering at the sight of it.

Then it disappears under the water.

I expect him to come to me.

Expect him to cover my body with his.

But he moves to the opposite side of the hot tub from me and lowers himself onto the seat.

Silently, we watch each other.

I take a large drink of my wine, and he pours himself another glass.

When he holds out the bottle, I hold out my glass, and I let him top it off.

I've heard the warnings. How mixing booze and hot tubs can be dangerous.

I've heard them, and I've ignored them.

But now that I'm here, finishing off my extra full glass, I think I understand.

Though I'm hardly discouraged from doing this again because even though we just ate, I feel... hungry.

Chapter Twenty-Nine

MICHAEL

Alice sets her empty glass down and slowly slides forward on her seat.

My dick hasn't gotten any softer since I got into the hot tub, and now, as she nears, it's getting impossibly harder.

Fingertips brush against my knees. "Will you do me a favor?"

Her voice is husky, and it sends a shiver down my spine. "Anything you want."

She runs her fingers up my thighs, stopping halfway. "Will you sit up on the edge?"

My stomach muscles clench. "Why?"

She drops her gaze to my lap, even though my arousal is hidden in the water.

"Because I'd like to suck your cock." She lifts her eyes back up to mine. "Please."

Chapter Thirty

ALICE

Michael lurches forward, capturing my face in his hands.

"You never have to say please for that, Mrs. Claus. You can put my dick in your mouth anytime you want."

Mrs. Claus shouldn't sound so hot, but after role-playing earlier, calling him Santa, the nickname hits me right in the chest.

Michael closes his mouth over mine.

We both open. Our tongues tasting the same. Like wine and lust and love.

I reach for him.

Cling to him.

He wraps his arms around me and pulls me against him.

My legs go on either side of his hips.

It's the same position we were in this morning, but the weightlessness of being in water means that I'm floating above his lap.

Michael utilizes this and moves his hand into the gap between us.

Blunt fingers slide between my folds.

Michael groans, finding me wet.

Then he pushes one of his fingers inside me, and my groan matches his.

My head swims.

Heat swirls around inside me.

And I rock my hips, fucking myself against his hand.

His lips never leave mine as he consumes my sounds.

Then something presses against my clit.

I think it's his thumb at first, then I realize it's bigger.

Much bigger.

I pull my head back and suck in a breath.

Michael has both hands between us. One with fingers buried inside me. The other gripping his cock and rubbing the head against my clit.

"Feel good?" he asks against my neck.

I moan and nod. "So, so good, Mr. Claus."

Teeth scrape against my skin. "Say that again."

"You feel so good, Mr. Claus." I dig my fingers into his shoulders, holding myself close, and I lean into the feeling of his cock against my clit.

"My Mrs." He increases the speed of his fingers moving in and out of me. "My pretty little Mrs. Claus getting herself off on the big man's lap."

His fingers twist inside me, and his cock presses into my clit just right. And my orgasm hits me like a snowball to the face.

I arch my back, my cry decorating the trees around us.

My body clenches.

My pussy squeezes his fingers.

And my heart triples in size.

"Mr. Claus," I pant. "I love you so much."

"Show me," Michael growls.

He pulls his hands free of my body and stands, stepping onto the footrest so his cock is just above the surface of the water.

His hands tangle in my hair. "Show me how much you love me."

Chapter Thirty-One

MICHAEL

Alice keeps her eyes on mine as she opens her mouth wide.

And when her pink tongue peeks out, I lose my last shred of control and surge my hips forward.

Chapter Thirty-Two

ALICE

Michael shoves his cock down my throat.

It's rough.

Frantic.

And perfect.

My eyes water.

I struggle to keep my throat muscles from seizing.

And I grip his thighs for balance.

"That's it." He pulls out and shoves back in. "Breathe through your nose, Baby Cakes. Just breathe and let me fucking take this throat."

I do.

I inhale and grip his legs tighter.

I blink at him.

I take in the primal look in his eyes.

And my core throbs.

"That's my girl." His cock almost slips free of my lips.

He pushes back in, his tip sliding even deeper this time.

"That's my good girl, earning her way back to the nice list."

Tears roll down my cheeks, pleasure and happiness swelling inside me.

Michael's hands flex in my hair, and the pull brings me right back to the edge.

I let go of him with one hand and reach down to that spot between my thighs.

The water has done nothing to wash away my slickness, and my fingers slip over my clit.

I moan around his length, and Michael uses his hold of my hair to pull me off his dick.

"Are you touching yourself, Little Alice?"

I nod, gasping for breath.

He drags my face forward, and I lick the slit at his tip.

Michael moans. "Rub that clit for me. I want you coming as you swallow me down."

I wrap my lips around the head of his dick, and he shoves his hips forward.

The sounds he's making...

The feeling of him filling my throat...

And my fingers on my already sensitive center...

I start to come, clamping my thighs together, trapping my hand in place even as I keep rubbing my clit.

"Fuck. That's it. Yeah, that's it, Baby. Come on those fingers." Michael jerks his hips forward.

His hands hold me still.

Holds himself deep in my throat.

"Now swallow."

It's the only warning I get.

His cock pulses in my mouth, and he starts to come.

I swallow.

I try to take it all.

But I'm not good at this.

It's too much.

I have to pull back, and his cock slips free from my mouth as I suck in a breath.

His hand is suddenly around his length, jerking it off, and the last two jets of release land across my lips and chin.

We're both panting.

Both gasping for breath.

I pull my hand out from between my thighs and grip his leg again.

"S-sorry," I heave.

Michael slowly shakes his head. "What the hell are you apologizing for?"

I reach up and run my fingers through the mess on my face. "I couldn't take it all."

Michael groans, and I watch as more release pulses from his cock. "You took fucking plenty."

I slide my fingers into my mouth, and Michael groans even louder, lowering himself into the water.

"Take anymore and you're gonna fucking kill me."

Chapter Thirty-Three

ALICE

Settled in my seat, I pull my phone out of my purse to put it in airplane mode and see I have a pair of missed calls, one from each of my cousins.

The flight attendant is already walking down the aisle, so instead of calling them back, I open our group chat and send them a text, letting them know we're about to take off and that I'll call when we get to our hotel.

Michael places his hand on my thigh as he leans his head back. "You okay?"

I tuck my phone away and place my hand over his. "I'm so okay."

The side of his mouth pulls up. "Good."

I lean my own head back. "Thank you for the best Christmas ever."

His fingers flex around my thigh. "Not something you need to thank me for, Sweetness."

"All the same." I let my eyes close.

With the short drive to the airport, we didn't have to get up early. But we stayed in the hot tub longer than we probably should have and then took our time showering off afterward.

Meaning we're both exhausted and I'm happy to nap my way to Vancouver.

Which is probably the smart call because I have a feeling things are going to turn up a notch when we get there.

Chapter Thirty-Four

MICHAEL

I'm used to people staring. It happens everywhere I go. But this...

I glance around as we walk through the Vancouver airport.

This is a little more attention than I normally get.

I tighten my hold on Alice's hand.

She glances up at me with a smile. "This airport is really nice."

I nod, agreeing, glad she doesn't seem to be stressing about all the eyes on us.

No doubt word has gotten out that I've made Alice mine.

I knew the photos taken in the Minneapolis airport would get around.

And I knew it would cause a buzz.

But I didn't think the good people of Canada would care this much.

A flash goes off to my right, and I let go of Alice's hand to drape my arm over her shoulders.

My protective instincts are flaring, and I need to settle down before I snap at someone and make an even bigger spectacle.

I spot a little convenience shop up ahead and steer Alice toward it.

"I'm gonna grab us some waters." I bend down a little so Alice can hear me. "We need to stay hydrated after travel."

"Probably smart." She bobs her head. "And I could go for a juice, if that's okay."

I hug her to my side. "Of course it's okay. Whatever you want, Baby."

I don't drop my arm until we're standing in front of the beverage coolers, then I use both hands to grab two large water bottles. "Grab whatever else you want. We'll order up some room service when we get to the hotel, but grab a snack now if you're hungry."

Alice grabs a bottle of cranberry juice. "Maybe just something small."

She turns to the racks behind us—with the granola bars, breath mints, and magazines.

Her juice idea actually sounds pretty good, so I shift both waters into one hand so I can grab my own.

My fingers are just about to graze the plastic when Alice lets out a choked cry.

My heart leaps into my throat, and I spin around, expecting to see someone accosting my woman.

But she's alone.

Standing only a few feet away from me.

Holding up one of the tabloid magazines.

"What is it?" I step up behind her.

"It's..." She lifts the tabloid, the paper shaking in her hands. "It's us."

Chapter Thirty-Five

ALICE

My mouth opens, but I don't know if I want to laugh, cry, or scream.

Because...

I close my mouth and swallow down the deranged sound that's trying to burst out of my lungs.

I read the caption below the photo.

While snowed in at Bear Cove, Chef Mike gets more than a Second Bite *of contestant Alice Hatter. More photos on page eight.*

More photos.

Meaning they have more photos than the large one printed across the front page of the cheap tabloid.

I move my eyes over the photo again, taking in the look of bliss on my face as the sun shines off my loose hair. My head tipped back. My hands digging into Michael's bare shoulders. His fingers... in my mouth.

"How?" I whisper.

How is there a photo of us mid-fuck on the kitchen chair?

It's graphic.

Lewd.

But you really can't see anything that you shouldn't. Except for Michael's bare back, his body blocking the front of mine.

And you can probably guess that he's sucking my nipple into his mouth, but you can't see it.

Something warm stirs in my center.

We look hot together.

"Turn to the other photos," Michael says with his chest against my back, looking over my shoulder.

I flip to page eight.

And this time I do make a sound.

Because that's Michael's dick in my mouth.

Chapter Thirty-Six

MICHAEL

I should not be getting hard right now.

I should not *be getting hard right now.*

But looking at a photo of my hands tangled in Alice's hair, her face just above the surface of the hot tub... It doesn't matter that they've blurred out the inches of visible cock between my body and her lips, it's clear what we're doing.

Crystal fucking clear.

I ignore the words printed on the page and look at the other photos.

Another of us in the hot tub, taken before the face-fucking moment, with Alice on my lap, my mouth on her neck, and enough body contact to know we're doing more than kissing.

The last photo is back in the kitchen.

And it's my bare ass.

I groan at that one.

Not exactly the image I've been crafting for myself over the past couple decades. But the sight of Alice's little feet digging into my back, pulling me closer, still has my cock thickening.

It's all pornographic, but Alice's naughty parts are covered in every image. All of the naked bits are mine.

Which is good because I'm going to ruin the photographer

when I find them. But if they'd shared more of Alice, I'd be ending their life, not just their career.

"What... I..." Alice croaks, and any stirring below my belt stops when it sounds like she might cry.

I step around her and crouch down, putting my face in front of hers.

A face that's biting down on a smile.

She slaps a hand over her mouth just as a laugh bubbles out.

"You're okay?" It's a stupid question, but I ask it anyway.

Alice lifts a shoulder. "I should probably be more horrified than I am."

"But?"

A peep of laughter slips out. "I can't help but notice how good we look."

I smirk. "They're pretty hot photos."

She nods, hand still over her mouth. "They are."

I pull Alice into a hug. "I love you, Baby. And I promise I'll take care of this."

Chapter Thirty-Seven

ALICE

A large black SUV with tinted windows pulls up in front of us.

A few more people were taking pictures of us as we passed through the airport to get our luggage, but I kept my gaze down and the tabloid tucked under my arm.

Michael presses his hand against my spine, urging me into the back seat of the SUV.

I go without protest, knowing that one of the show producers is the one picking us up.

The producer, a.k.a. driver, helps Michael get our bags into the back, then they both climb in, Michael in the back next to me.

"So," the producer starts as he pulls away from the curb, "you two sure know how to make an entrance."

Michael just grunts, but my worry starts to kick in.

"Is this, um, situation, going to ruin anything for *Second Bite?*" I have to ask.

The producer laughs. "Hell no. Our projected viewership just shot through the roof."

My eyes widen. "Seriously? Why?"

"Because." The producer glances over his shoulder at me. "Pamela got sick and can't make it to the recording."

"Pamela," I whisper the name of the woman who always judges beside Michael.

The man nods. "Yep. And we just announced you as her replacement."

ABOUT THE AUTHOR

Like all her books, S. J. Tilly resides in the glorious state of Minnesota, where she was born and raised. To avoid the freezing cold winters, S. J. enjoys burying her head in books, whether to read them or write them or listen to them.

When she's not busy writing her contemporary smut, she can be found lounging with her husband and their herd of rescue boxers. And when the weather permits, she loves putting her compost to use in the garden, pretending to know what she's doing. The neighbors may not like the flowery mayhem of her yard, but the bees sure do. And really, that's more important.

To stay up to date on all things Tilly, make sure to follow her on her socials, join her newsletter, and interact whenever you feel like it! Links to everything on her website www.sjtilly.com

ALSO BY S.J. TILLY

Love Letters Series

Contemporary Romance

Love, Utley

Hannah

Maddox Lovelace. The captivating football player I met in college.

The one I only knew for a week. A week that was... life-changing.

Until my phone rang, and I had no choice but to go home.

I left Maddox a letter, putting my feelings on paper, giving him my number, hoping he'd call.

But he didn't call.

He never called.

He got drafted into the professional league and lived like a king while I stayed home and struggled to stay afloat.

I may have followed his career, but now that he's retired from football, I've forced myself to stop thinking about him.

And it's okay that I won't ever see him again. That week in college was fifteen years ago.

I'm not in love with Maddox anymore.

I might even hate him.

Maddox

Hannah Utley. The name that's haunted me since my senior year of college.

The girl who caught my attention with her wide eyes and freckled nose.

Who spent one week twisting up my insides until she stole a piece of my heart the night we got locked inside the campus library.

The girl who disappeared without a word.

It's the name of the girl I've been trying to forget for fifteen years.

And it's the name looking up at me from the résumé in my hand.

Because Hannah Utley works for the company I just purchased.

And that makes her mine. Whether she likes it or not.

Tackled in the Stacks

I caught her staring at me from across the quad, eyes fixed on the football jersey stretched across my wide chest. And if I flexed my muscles, showing off the strength of a defensive tackle, it was just to see her blush.

And then she did, and I couldn't get her out of my mind.

Her wide eyes. The freckles on her cheeks.

I needed to know her. The girl who scampered away every time we bumped into each other—by accident and by design. The girl who shyly agreed to come to my game, getting her first taste of football. The girl, Hannah Utley, who worked at the campus library and let me rest my head on her shoulder as she read to me in one of the study rooms.

It was innocent. Mostly.

Until we lose track of time and discover that the library has closed. And we're locked inside.

Now it's me and Hannah in the stacks.

Alone.

With nothing but desire between us.

Alliance Series

Dark Mafia Romance

NERO

Payton

Running away from home at seventeen wasn't easy. Let's face it, though, nothing before, or in the ten years since, has ever been easy for me.

And I'm doing okay. Sorta. I just need to keep scraping by, living under the radar. Staying out of people's way, off people's minds.

So when a man walks through my open patio door, stepping boldly into my home and my life, I should be scared. Frightened. Terrified.

But I must be more broken than I realized because I'm none of those things.

I'm intrigued.

And I'm wondering if the way to take control of my life is by giving in to him.

Nero

The first time I took a man's life, I knew there'd be no going back. No normal existence in the cards for me.

So instead of walking away, I climbed a mountain of bodies and created my own destiny. By forming The Alliance.

And I was fine with that. Content enough to carry on.

Until I stepped through those open doors and into her life.

I should've walked away. Should've gone right back out the door I came through. But I didn't.

And now her life is in danger.

But that's the thing about being a bad man. I'll happily paint the streets red to protect what's mine.

And Payton is mine. Whether she knows it or not.

KING

Okay, so, my bad for assuming the guy I was going on a date with *wasn't* married. And my bad for taking him to a friend's house for dinner, only to find out my friend is also friends with *his* wife. Because, in fact, he *is* married. And she happens to be at my friend's house because her husband was *busy working*.

Confused? So am I.

Unsurprisingly, my date's wife is super angry about finding out that her husband is a cheating asshole.

Girl, I get it.

Then, to make matters more convoluted, there is the man sitting next to my date's wife. A man named King, who is apparently her brother and who lives up to his name.

And since my *date* is a two-timing prick, I'm not going to feel bad about drooling over King,

especially since I'll never see him again.

Or at least I don't plan to.

I plan to take an Uber to the cheater's apartment to get my car keys.

I plan for it to be quick.

And if I had to list a thousand possible outcomes... witnessing my date's murder, being kidnapped by his killer, and then being forced to marry the super attractive but clearly

deranged crime lord would not have been on my Bingo card.

But alas, here I am.

DOM

VAL

When I was nine, I went to my first funeral. Along with accepting my father's death, I had to accept new and awful truths I wasn't prepared for.

When I was nineteen, I went to my mother's funeral. We weren't close, but with her gone, I became more alone than ever before.

Sure, I have a half brother who runs The Alliance. And yeah, he's given me his protection—in the form of a bodyguard and chauffeur. But I don't have anyone that really knows me. No one to really love me.

Until I meet him. The man in the airport.

And when one chance meeting turns into something hotter, something more serious, I let myself believe that maybe he's the one. Maybe this man is the one who will finally save me from my loneliness. The one to give me the family I've always craved.

DOM

The Mafia is in my blood. It's what I do.

So when that blood is spilled and one funeral turns into three, drastic measures need to be taken.

And when this battle turns into a war, I'm going to need more men. More power.

I'm going to need The Alliance.

And I'll become a member. By any means necessary.

HANS

Vengeance is rarely clean.

Sin Series

Romantic Suspense

Mr. Sin

I should have run the other way. Paid my tab and gone back to my room. But he was there. And he was... everything. I figured, what's the harm in letting passion rule my decisions for one night? So what if he looks like the Devil in a suit? I'd be leaving in the morning. Flying home, back to my pleasant but predictable life. I'd never see him again.

Except I do. In the last place I expected. And now everything I've worked so hard for is in jeopardy.

We can't stop what we've started, but this is bigger than the two of us.

And when his past comes back to haunt him, love might not be enough to save me.

Sin Too

Beth

It started with tragedy.

And secrets.

Hidden truths that refused to stay buried have come out to chase me. Now I'm on the run, living under a blanket of constant fear, pretending to be someone I'm not. And if I'm not really me, how am I supposed to know what's real?

Angelo

Watch the girl.

It was supposed to be a simple assignment. But like everything else in this family, there's nothing simple about it. Not my task. Not her fake name. And not my feelings for her.

But Beth is mine now.

So when the monsters from her past come out to play, they'll have to get through me first.

Miss Sin

I'm so sick of watching the world spin by. Of letting people think I'm plain and boring, too afraid to just be myself.

Then I see *him*.

John.

He's strength and fury and unapologetic.

He's everything I want. And everything I wish I was.

He won't want me, but that doesn't matter. The sight of him is all the inspiration I need to finally shatter this glass house I've built around myself.

Only he does want me. And when our worlds collide, details we can't see become tangled, twisting together, ensnaring us in an invisible trap.

When it all goes wrong, I don't know if I'll be able to break free of the chains binding us or if I'll suffocate in the process.

Sleet Series

Hockey Romantic Comedy

Sleet Kitten

There are a few things that life doesn't prepare you for. Like what to do when a super-hot guy catches you sneaking around in his basement. Or what to do when a mysterious package shows up with tickets to a hockey game, because apparently, he's a professional athlete. Or how to handle it when you get to the game and realize he's freaking famous since half of the 20,000 people in the stands are wearing his jersey.

I thought I was a well-adjusted adult, reasonably prepared for life. But one date with Jackson Wilder, a viral video, and a "I didn't know she was your mom" incident, and I'm suddenly questioning everything I thought I knew.

But he's fun. And great. And I think I might be falling for him. But I don't know if he's falling for me too, or if he's as much of a player off the ice as on.

Sleet Sugar

My friends have convinced me. No more hockey players.

With a dad who is the head coach for the Minnesota Sleet, it seemed like an easy decision.

My friends have also convinced me that the best way to boost my fragile self-esteem is through a one-night stand.

A dating app. A hotel bar. A sexy-as-hell man, who's sweet and funny, and did I mention, sexy as hell... I fortified my courage and invited myself up to his room.

Assumptions. There's a rule about them.

I assumed he was passing through town. I assumed he was a businessman or maybe an investor or accountant or literally anything other than a professional hockey player. I assumed I'd never see him again.

I assumed wrong.

Sleet Banshee

Mother-freaking hockey players. My friends found their happily ever afters with a couple of sweet, doting, over-the-top, in-love athletes. They got nicknames like *Kitten* and *Sugar*. But me? I got stuck with a dickhead who riles me up on purpose and calls me *Banshee*. Yeah, he might have a voice made specifically for wet dreams. And he might have a body and face carved by the gods. And he might have a level of Alpha-hole that gets me all hot and bothered.

But when he presses my buttons, he presses ALL of my buttons. And

I'm not the type of girl who takes things sitting down. And I only got caught on my knees that one time. In the museum.

But when one of my decisions gets one of my friends hurt... I can't stop blaming myself. And him.

Except he can't take a hint. And I can't keep my panties on.

Darling Series

Contemporary Small Town Romance

Smoky Darling

Elouise

I fell in love with Beckett when I was seven.

He broke my heart when I was fifteen.

When I was eighteen, I promised myself I'd forget about him.

And I did. For a dozen years.

But now he's back home. Here. In Darling Lake. And I don't know if I should give in to the temptation swirling between us or run the other way.

Beckett

She had a crush on me when she was a kid. But she was my brother's best friend's little sister. I didn't see her like that. And even if I had, she was too young. Our age difference was too great.

But now I'm back home. And she's here. And she's all the way grown up.

It wouldn't have worked back then. But I'll be damned if I won't get a taste of her now.

Latte Darling

I have a nice life—living in my hometown, owning the coffee shop I've worked at since I was sixteen.

It's comfortable.

On paper.

But I'm tired of doing everything by myself. Tired of being in charge of every decision in my life.

I want someone to lean on. Someone to spend time with. Sit with. Hug.

And I really don't want to go to my best friend's wedding alone.

So, I signed up for a dating app and agreed to meet with the first guy who messaged me.

And now here I am, at the bar.

Only it's not my date that just sat down in the chair across from me. It's his dad.

And holy hell, he's the definition of silver fox. If a silver fox can be thick as a house, have piercing blue eyes and tattoos from his neck down to his fingertips.

He's giving me *big bad wolf* vibes. Only instead of running, I'm blushing. And he looks like he might just want to eat me whole.

Tilly World Holiday Novellas

Second Bite

When a holiday baking competition goes incredibly wrong. Or right...

Michael

I'm starting to think I've been doing this for too long. The screaming fans. The constant media attention. The fat paychecks. None of it brings me the happiness I yearn for.

Yet here I am. Another year. Another holiday special. Another Christmas spent alone in a hotel room.

But then the lights go up. And I see *her.*

Alice

It's an honor to be a contestant, I know that. But right now, it feels a little like punishment. Because any second, Chef Michael Kesso, the man I've been in love with for years, the man who doesn't even know I exist, is going to walk onto the set, and it will be a miracle if I don't pass out at the sight of him.

But the time for doubts is over. Because *Second Bite* is about to start "in three... two... one..."